The Ting Behind 2
(Is More Than 3)

Lovette Tucker

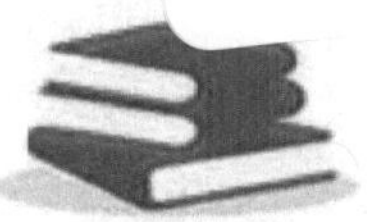

Liberia\ USA\ Thailand

First Published in 2020
Published by:

FORTE Publications
#12 Ashmun Street
Snapper Hill
Monrovia, Liberia
[+231] 777155-923
[+231] 881-106-177

FORTE Publishing
7202 Tavenner Lane
208 Alexandria
VA, 22306

FORTE Press
76 Sarasit Road
Ban Pong, 70110
Ratchaburi, Thailand
[+66] 85-824-4382

http://fortepublishing.wix.com/fppp
fortepublishing@gmaill.com

Dedication

To my mother,
Bertha Baker Azango.

"The ting behind 2 more than 3" was a colloquial phrase used by my mother whenever she gave advice or answered questions of "why". Her response usually meant that the answer was more complicated than what we thought.

Acknowledgement

Liberians are beautiful, happy people. There is much laughter and fun among us. Even with the trauma of war, the scare of Ebola, the disappointment with leadership, the lack of economic prowess among the nations of the world, the extreme poverty and all the negatives, we still manage to smile, giggle or give a good laugh.

This book is dedicated to Liberians. Keep laughing!

Contents

Chapter One

"People of stature do not emerge in a vacuum. They are influenced by culture, environmental, psychosocial, economic, and other factors."

Bertha Baker Azango
in *Image & Influence* (2015)

A NEW DAWN

Here I sit, listening to the evening news on the radio. I'm hearing what we've all known since... well last week! There will be a change in this situation.

I live in a rural area where people are going on about their businesses. Music is blaring from the club nearby as they prepare for the night of rabblerousing. The pehn-pehn boys on their bikes go, *vroom, vroom* down the street. It's a typical night, not too loud but not quiet either. One's ears tend to get used to the sounds of the night in this faraway place.

With so many young people around there's bound to be loud talking and posturing. Young men saying "Come here" to the girls and they, in turn, giggling about lord knows what.

"Why should I come?"

"Oh, you geh, stop bluffing and come mehn."

"You nah ready yet. When you want see me, you wey stop acting."

Just then, someone yelled, "Jor Weah na win oh!" He excitedly ran towards his friends and together they clapped hands and laughed and jumped around a bit in circles. They feel they have done a good thing. I don't hear much more because I moved to the back of the house.

During the week, there were these little puddles of water from the rain. Throughout the night, we heard heavy beats on the roof due to falling rain. Each night I went to bed thinking, "Is this an omen of things to come? Is this God crying or is He cleansing? Sadly, one can never know the mind of God."

Each night, though, I say my prayers and ask God to bless this land and the people in it. When you've lived as long as I have you feel like you've been here before.

Things change but things stay the same.

The next day I decide to go into town. I need to get supplies and I have my grocery list. As I head out the door, I remember to check the lights.

Checking the lights means going through the kitchen to make sure that I switch the breaker from generator electricity to city electricity. Then I check the stove to make sure that I have not left it turned on. A quick look around the kitchen shows that the refrigerator is slightly ajar, so I bang it shut. Then I close the pantry door. Satisfied that all is well, I then move to the bedroom to check that I have plugged in the battery pack so that if the city electricity returns while I am out, my battery will be fully charged.

My phone is charged so I am assured that it will last until I come back from shopping. I take one more look around the house, lock the door and I am ready. I don't take my umbrella because the sun is shining bright. Once more, a prayer of thanks that Jehovah God has spared my life and that the day will be bright.

Next Day

I read an analysis by Dr. Patrick Burrowes. It is insightful and right on the money. It puts into words what I heard during the campaign. Dr. Burrowes said that in "Kolokwa", the young people were speaking out. They were opting for morality, compassion, virtue and consistency over what they view as corruption and selfishness.

This is such an eye opener for me. I had already felt, during the campaign and before, that as an intellectual, I should be rooting for leadership and experience.

During the first round, I looked for a candidate who had shown love for country (as it turned out they all did) and had resumes, which showed they had "managed" organizations and businesses. I thought everyone felt as I did that one needed experience and intellect to govern a country. After all, it was obvious. I was a little taken aback when the names of the top two were mentioned. But I said to myself that I needed to move on and pick a likely winner. And so I forged ahead.

This is a country that, according to the last census, has a population of over 4 million persons. Within the 4 million, over 65% are identified as youth. This means that there are over 2.5 million persons who are under the age of 35. That's a staggering number of people. They have been trying to talk since the war was over but, as is often the case, we tend to congregate and socialize with those of our own ilk.

Therefore, the "youth" congregate with their peers, their friends and the older folk congregate likewise.

They feel that even though they have articulated what they are interested in (think jobs, security, and equality), things don't seem to be going their way. Unemployment is up, especially in that group and many are labeled as "Zogos", a derogatory term for those who cause trouble.

People throw around words like disenfranchised and uncultured. I know what that means in a more developed nation. Certain people feel like they have been sidelined. They are not included in the decisions that affect them.

Once when I was at a shop and the youthful patrons were talking politics I asked them "Why would you vote for Weah?" The guy said that because he felt he owed Weah for the loyalty that Weah had shown to Liberia. He felt that during what he called the dark days of the war Weah was a shining light who showed that Liberians could be more than just warlords.

Weah showed the world that something good could come out of Liberia. I remember during those dark days, Liberians, both in and out of Liberia, hung their heads in shame. Many people wondered, "Are these Liberians doing these type of atrocities? Can these be the same people who love a good party, hanging with friends and lecturing, the same people who are killing and maiming each other?"

These questions lingered around for 20 years with all trying to understand this phenomenon.

What makes one turn from being a good natured, loyal being into a killer (barring the influence of drugs and other antisocial chemical inducers)? I don't want to get into the reasons for the war at this point suffice to say that greed and the thirst for power became two important factors in prolonging the war and suffering.

After 2005 we craved the absence of war which we received.

What we did not factor in was the carpetbaggers moving in. They came from all corners of the globe. They weren't only Liberians. They were people of all races and creeds.

They saw a wounded deer and like a bunch of rabid wolves they encircled their prey, intent on devouring the meat. Instead of bullets and cannons they brought money because their prey feasted on the gods of materialism. The carpetbagger is the term in American history which refers to the persons who came from the north to the south after the civil war. These were the "nouveau rich". They had money and were willing to pick up the spoils of war for cheap. In the case of Liberia, the thing called corruption reared its ugly head.

Corruption is the most feared element of Liberian society. Corruption has permeated the nation from the highest level to the little children.

Almost anything intangible can be bought in Liberia. So let's delve into what is corruption in Liberia.

Corruption has two sides. The gasoline that powers corruption is called family. In Liberia, family extends beyond the usual nucleus family made up of parents and siblings. It even goes further than family as described in the western sense when you include cousins, aunts and uncles.

Imagine the net, stretched even further to include the maternal and the paternal sides of the family, and you've got a big group. In Liberia, family entails an even bigger net than that. In historical terms, the country was made up of small hamlets and villages. Everyone in the village was considered family. Later, the villages became towns and the towns became cities. The idea of family did not restrict itself but rather included everyone in the town. These relationships with family is what pushes people into doing things they would not normally do.

A family member goes to the bank and needs to be served so he calls up a family member to do the task even though there are people who have been waiting a long time for the service.

A student does not make high marks in a community school so the parents appeal to the family member to make the grades better. People expect to be treated favorably in business dealings because they are "family" by association.

Family may also include a friend of a friend. I've heard people complain that they make little money but they need to support their family so if the paycheck is not enough and there is some means to get money, it's morally all right.

Today, I realize that it should not matter that much who leads this country. I should focus on the biblical theme of loving my neighbor. I have to define what that means for me. All my life I have been a teacher or played a mentor role to young people, even my own children.

This is what I feel comfortable doing so this must be my neighborhood. We all need to find our neighbor, whether it is a cause, a group of people, or a service. Once you determine your neighbor then you must focus on loving your neighbor. Love in this sense means doing the things that bring your neighbor to a greater place, not pull them down.

Liberia can emerge from the ashes of war and corruption. We have what it takes in us individually and collectively to move beyond petty jealousies and ignorance. We must take the high road. This means we much look to each other for what is good in us and don't focus so much on the negative.

John is mean but John is also a good father. See the good in people and allow them to see the good in you. Love your neighbor and the rest will take care of itself.

Chapter Two

Aye, jeh becor Tamba Is Not In Foya so he na no natin…

This is one of those 21st century Liberianisms that is only recently being widely allowed and used in our vernacular. It is similar to the western story, *Alice in Wonderland,* where Alice found herself in a different place from where she came, Kansas. In the story, "Alice is not in Kansas anymore". The implication being, she had to think and act differently because she was in a new place.

The Tamba implication is similar and yet dissimilar.

The story goes that *Tamba was away from Foya[1], his hometown. He got into a fight with another boy and the boy was beating Tamba up. Tamba struggled to get a break,*

---

[1] Foya/Foyah is a rather large city in Lofa county, the northwest of Liberia.

backed away from the boy, panting and crying. Tamba then said, "You only beating me because we not in Foya! Hmm. If we were in Foya, I swear, I will be beating you." (Laughter ensued from onlookers).

*****

My daughter, Love, is a wonderful, caring person. She is quite dedicated to her family and her studies. In her final year at the university where Love was studying to be a nurse, an incident occurred.

One time my sister came to visit. She complained of a headache, so we called Love to get her some medicine. She came, brought the medicine, gave it to my sister, and went to get some water.

I said to Love, "Aren't you supposed to be finding out what's wrong with her by asking her some questions? You just came and gave the medicine to her. I can do that and I'm not a nurse. What are you learning that you are doing the same thing that a non-nurse would do!

Love said, "But Mammie, we're not in the hospital. In the hospital, we ask the patients their background but this is the house and she is not a patient. She is Auntie."

My sister said, "Oh. Because, Tamba is not in Foya now so he can't do anything!"

We both burst out into laughter.

I must say, we teased her mercilessly. I said, "Four years of nursing education and here you come and just hand her the medicine."

She said, "But that's the one she asked for!"

"So does the patient just come in the hospital and tell the doctor which treatment to give?"

Anyway, Love did the right thing. She began to ask the right questions and even attempted to complete an intake form!

****

Tamba is not in Foyah.

We had a fellow who drove us from Gbarnga to Monrovia. Gbarnga is a rural community while Monrovia is an urban center with four lane roads and many choices of turns. The driver was fine going from Gbarnga. It is a two-lane road and the driver was fine. His name, coincidentally, was Tamba.

As soon as we got to Monrovia, Tamba got confused. We had to tell him to go into the next lane when the lane he was in, was moving too slow or had stopped. We had to direct him to take streets other than the one he had driven before to get to where we were going.

The funny thing is Tamba always answered "Yes" when we asked him if he knew where to go. He never admitted that he didn't know where he was, until the end, when we had harassed him enough about not being able to drive in the city.

"Mmm, mmm! Tamba is not in Foyah anymore." We'd say something to the effect and laugh.

****

Throughout life, we get into unfamiliar situations – a new love, a new job, a new school. Change is the only constant we have. Things will change. We grow up, we die, etc. The important thing is how we deal with that change.

There were some, during the war years, that had to flee their homes and all that was familiar. They went into new and strange places. Some thrived and others did not. What made the difference?

Those who thrived recognized that they had baggage but they had to compartmentalize the pain and struggle of war. They had to push all of the negatives aside. They had to, as they say, *put on their big girl panties* and move on. They had to wise up, be adults, and move on.

Some did not thrive. Why? My reasoning is that, these people, for whatever reason, could not leave behind the baggage. They had family members, wealth, or property that they needed to manage.

The baggage was constantly on their minds and they could not focus on the now. These people were the ones who came alive in gatherings that spoke of the war because they had huge opinions.

They were the loudest voices about "Liberia" and "Liberians". They were strong in their convictions in discussions about what to do back home.

In turn, they had narrow ideas of the places where they resided. Because they spent so much time and effort focusing on the past, they did not relish the future.

As a result, they floundered in the new. They reacted in ways that dragged them. They addressed their situations in ways that only brought them pain and depression.

For them, Tamba was not in Foyah anymore, hence, he could not play or do any of his regular activities – including live- well!

They just didn't live or should I say play well?

Chapter Three

Dry dog sweet but what will you be eating while you waiting for the dog to get dried?

This was especially funny (and gross!) when I first heard it. Who eats dried dog? I know that in my neck of the woods, dogs were pets, not food so the idea of eating dog meat was especially foreign to me.

During the war, people had to eat whatever they could find, and that included dog meat. So even though it may have seemed abhorrent so some, they had to learn to live with. Anyway, substitute any other type of meat for the word dog that will make it more palatable to you – chicken, beef, pork, and fish. Any of these can be dried and they all will take a while to get done. So the main point of the saying is "What do you eat while you are waiting for the fish to get dried?"

Promises, promises. In the West they learn to curb hunger for impulse buying through the use of credit or credit cards. They buy things they don't need because they want to impress people or because it is their habit.

It is also because they don't think through what they already have before they purchase. They don't have to wait for the fulfillment of the promise because they can get it on credit. Once they've bought the item via credit or credit cards, then there is the *regret* phase, because now, they have to look at the bills and their actual cash flow, but it's too late.

In Liberia, mostly, our shops are not overloaded with goods that one just has to have. That can be a good thing because it means that people tend to buy less impulsively. They have to wait until there is enough money and the circumstances are right; but they have to wait, and that is what this brand of Liberianism alludes to.

However, we know too well that waiting is tough. The Bible speaks all the time about "waiting on the Lord" but that is a hard thing to do when there are so many other things, right in front of our noses, demanding immediate attention.

As a child, you are often told to wait until you get older, bigger, or matured. It may be true that the dried meat sweet, well-seasoned and better preserved, but rarely do they tell you what to do in the interim. What do I do while the meat is getting dried? This for me is a serious problem. We need to do more than just telling.

As a parent and teacher, I understand the need to make children wait. I know what the end is going to be but they may not. I know that the light at the end of the tunnel is a fast moving train, so I want to shield the little ones from certain disaster.

Oh, but they are impatient. They want it now, in fact, they want it like yesterday. This impulsiveness may also lead to corruption; a kind that I think is an even bigger societal sore. If people feel denied for many years for various reasons – lack of education and health services, lack of money, they nurture a sense of desperation that is hard to explain.

Thus, when they get to a place where they have power over these things, their impatient minds tell them that there is no need to wait any longer. They must have it now. That idea of newness, plus a sense of entitlement – because they suffered their way to this point - often lead to theft, robbery, and even murder. Yes, some people would even kill to get those things they have lacked.

My take on this Liberianism is that it is a two-edged sword. On the one hand, we live in a society without a credit system that is cumbersome at best and where promises by employers, private or public, are often left unfulfilled. People are forced to ask, on a daily basis, the question "What must I do while the meat is getting dried?"

Yes. What must I do while awaiting the fulfillment of a promise?

Therefore, people, who loudly proclaim a belief in an almighty power greater than themselves, resort to depending on themselves.

Even though they go to a place or worship at least once a week, they tend to compartmentalize their religiosity and their reality. Or they build a disconnect between *Dry Dog Sweet* (future) and *this is what I'll be eating until the dog is dried* (now). They lie, cheat, or steal so easily to get the now.

The other edge of the sword comes with the danger of their actions. Either on a greater scale or individually, they fail to see how their actions perpetually place others in the society in the same position from which, they have just left.

They whine about ills when in the bucket but are the first ones to defecate inside the bucket when they rise up to the rim. They become that which they detested. Ironic ain't it?

The general attitude is nonchalance at best. The laughter at the end of the phrase, solidifies the beliefs, *Don't credit anyone, Don't wait for someone to pay you later. Take your money up front,* because you don't know what will happen in the end.

****

This is less a sermon than it is an advice, which is what the Liberianism is intended to do.

Chapter Four

"I nah killing myseh for nobahly busney."

My aunty Yede is the quintessential organizer. When there is an event that needs planning, she takes the lead. For family reunions, Aunty Yede schedules the conference calls and gets everyone in line. Aunty Yede calls us when family members pass away. She tells us who will bring the food, who will pay monies and who will do what. She is always a reliable source of information. Once she is around, things tend to fall into place.

So what's the issue?

Well, one day while at my house, I naturally assumed that Aunty Yede would give me direction or at least offer an opinion, give advice, or do one of what *is expected* of her. She looked squarely at me and said, "No!"

I was confused. "Huh?" I felt like she was being unreasonable. Rather sheepishly (because I didn't want to be disrespectful) I said, "Why?"

She said, "I have arrived". Again I looked at her questioningly. Well, what I expected honestly was that she would say she was tired or "later". After all, I had asked nicely. Also, I was merely asking out of respect.

I fully expected her to provide me with what I needed at the time I needed it, which was *right now*. I mean, wasn't I her darling niece? Aren't old people just wired that way? Wasn't she supposed to give me guidance and be a strong shoulder to lean on? Isn't that what the older folks should do for the younger ones? As you can imagine I was in a huff.

I was pleasant (as much as I could be in my hurtful, rejected state) for the rest of the afternoon. I determined that I wasn't going to ask her to do one more thing for me. If she wanted to be that way, then two could play that game.

Later, despite my anger, I asked Aunty Yede what that meant, "I have arrived".

She stared at me with that *Chah, you belleh lee me lone* look and said, "It means I don't have to do ANYTHING I DON'T want to do. I do not HAVE to DO anything!"

Just like that, she went back to *arriving*. The finality, with which she said it, left no room for argument.

Well that was that! I pondered over that phrase for a long time. As children from "good" upbringings, you don't say "no" to anybody unless they're younger than you. The most common word in your vocabulary from ages 5 to 16 is "Yes" or other variations of it, i.e. "yes ma'am", "okay" or just "yeah" (in which case be prepared for a reprimand). This word is said to parents, teachers and anyone else at the school - preachers, older siblings, and the list goes on.

Imagine, for most of your life, while living under "their" roof, they have told you what to do and how to live, and then poof! You're an adult, more or less, and you've lived in child mode for so long, now, it is the most comfortable place to be. It can be a difficult transition for some.

****

Being an adult has been great. It's like eating chocolate from both ends.

As a mother, I have had more experience than my children. So for them, I am this fountain of knowledge.

"Wear your jacket because it will be cold later".

"Don't play near the stove. There's hot stuff on there and you'll get burned".

"Your first breakup? Don't worry. There are other fishes in the sea".

For the girls, "Don't let anyone touch you under your clothes. Boys want ONE thing. Once you give in, they're gone".

For the boys, "Respect women like they're your mother".

I make myself available because, as a young mother there were older people like my parents, aunts, uncles, and many others who were a phone call away that I could run to for help. Even my priests were always older.

You can begin to understand why this new rigmarole that aunty Yede had put me in was worrisome. What was I to think or do now?

I have arrived.

The sting of that simple line still cuts when I recall the moment I first heard it. But when I consider her explanation, it feels better. It is no longer as annoying as before.

Years later, I realize how amazingly empowering her simple words are. I know now that my Aunty provided me with a gift. In essence, what she said was, "I'm living my life for me. For too long I have been the one others have leaned on; the go-to person. The ones I leaned on are gone for the most part. I have to lean on me."

Now I have to reorient my thinking. I have to figure out what matters to me. I have to do what is best for me. I have to give me, as much *me* time. It doesn't mean I have to be selfish, just that, I have to place me on top of the care list.

Chapter Five

Catfish can't come from under the water and tell you alligator head hurting and you say that's a lie.

When you [an older person] tell a small boy "Dah pahnkana (palmnuts) you bussing, pupu insah oh."

The boy says "Oh Ma, Wait yah. I looking at aye. No pupu deh."

When she insists, the boy says "Leave me yah. Yor ley old pepo, yor like to talk."

But when he bursts open the pahnkana and the pupu flashes on his face he says "Old ma, da true you wor talking oh," but by then he's got pupu all over him.

You see, it is already late.

When older people hear this Liberianism and say "Um hmmm! Yes" because they know exactly where their friend is coming from.

They laugh and slap their thighs and tie their lappa tighter. They too know the deepness of the message.

Young people can be daredevils. They have no fear. They do things without measuring the consequences.

It must be their underdeveloped brain cells that cannot grasp the entirety of the situation. Or some other urge to prove a point or just youth.

When I think of some of things I participated in as a young person, I cringe because now I know there is no way I could ever attempt those things.

As a young miss I got on a plane going to America with a friend. The fare included a stop in Europe where one could get out and go into the city for about a week. The only caveat was that you had to return to the same airport to get on a flight going to your final destination. Can you imagine!

We got off in Amsterdam, a city of legal drugs, drinking and sex, and strolled around for at least a weekend. Of course we did not get into all of that but just the idea that we did, scares me.

Of course, Marilyn was more adventurous than I was and I bet she had more fun.

There was another time I went to Las Vegas (the gambling Mecca) and went looking around without a chaperone.

I mean, I moved from casino to casino without watching my back. As they say, I didn't have a care in the world. I'm sure all of us have had those experiences.

Aye yah! When you don't know, you don't know. Those can be fun times!

Now I know it's what old people are thinking when they sit by themselves and are just laughing. The young people don't understand what's going on but one day they will, by and by.

As an older person, one sometimes hesitates to give advice. Perhaps you've been belittled in the past. "Old ma, moo fron here yah! Your time is over." You can't stop, though. The young have to learn from the mistakes and successes of the older generation. That's how it was done in your day and how it's supposed to be. Let them open the pahnkana and let the pupu flash on their faces, then they will learn. And we will sit back, tie our lappas tighter, and just smile; maybe eve laugh.

Chapter Six

THE "TING" BEHIND 2, MORE THAN 3

"Ley ting you nah know, older than you."

It is a mathematical fact that when you count, one, two, the next whole number is three. So what exactly did my mother mean by the *ting behind two more than three*[2]?

No, she wasn't counting. She was delivering a message. I don't

---

[2] *The thing behind two is more than three,* is a Liberian proverb.

remember the first time she said it though, but she always did.

My mother was a quiet woman of insight. She threw in these snippets of wisdom any chance she got. This was preceded by those motherly "Hmmms!" Or "mmhmms!" usually followed by a short grunt. (Did I spell that so you understand?)

Anyway, when she said it, I always smiled in a condescending way." Weh day (What is this) Oldma talking about again?"

****

****

When a student in my current line of work brings me an explanation, I think about this phrase. "There's more to this story". Go deeper. Invariably, the first story is not the entire truth. One has to go beyond the story and look at all sides. In this respect, I almost feel like a preacher. You know how they take one or two pieces of scripture like "Jesus Wept." or "It is finished." and create a whole sermon that lasts anywhere from 20 minutes to an hour?

I mean, they take you into the passage, around it and by the time they are done, you are drawn to a conclusion that you had no idea about before you entered that pew.

Wow! How does one gain such a varied perspective about events?

****

Read the following story of **Blind Men and the Elephant – A Poem by John Godfrey Saxe.**

Here is John Godfrey Saxe's (1816-1887) version of *Blind Men and the Elephant:*

It was six men of Indostan,
To learning much inclined,
Who went to see the Elephant
(Though all of them were blind),
That each by observation
Might satisfy his mind.

The *First* approach'd the Elephant,
And happening to fall
Against his broad and sturdy side,
At once began to bawl:
"God bless me! but the Elephant
Is very like a wall!"

The *Second,* feeling of the tusk,
Cried, -"Ho! What have we here
So very round and smooth and
sharp?
To me 'tis mighty clear,
This wonder of an Elephant
Is very like a spear!"

The *Third* approach'd the animal,
And happening to take
The squirming trunk within his
hands,
Thus boldly up and spake:
"I see," -quoth he- "the Elephant
Is very like a snake!"

The *Fourth* reached out an eager
hand,
And felt about the knee:
"What most this wondrous beast is
like
Is mighty plain," -quoth he,-
"'Tis clear enough the Elephant
Is very like a tree!"
The *Fifth*, who chanced to touch the
ear,
Said- "E'en the blindest man
Can tell what this resembles most;
Deny the fact who can,
This marvel of an Elephant
Is very like a fan!"

The *Sixth* no sooner had begun
About the beast to grope,
Then, seizing on the swinging tail
That fell within his scope,
"I see," -quoth he, - "the Elephant
Is very like a rope!"

And so these men of Indostan
Disputed loud and long,
Each in his own opinion
Exceeding stiff and strong,
Though each was partly in the right,
And all were in the wrong![3]

---

[3]According to Wikipedia (https://en.wikipedia.org/wiki/Blind_men_and_an_elephant), culled on July 4, 2017, "The earliest versions of the parable of blind men and elephant is found in Buddhist, Hindu and Jain texts, as they discuss the limits of perception and the importance of complete context"

MORAL

So, oft in theologic wars
The disputants, I ween,
Rail on in utter ignorance
Of what each other mean;
And prate about an Elephant
Not one of them has seen!

****

Nowadays when I say this to the younger folks, what I mean is look beyond your circumstance. Look to the future.

It's funny that here at my school, I usually ask the question of all graduating seniors, "What are your plans for the day after graduation, the day after the party and the day after the hangover?" (Graduations are usually held on a weekend day).

Invariably, I get one of two answers. "Old ma, we're looking up to you (older guys) to help us to find jobs."

Or "I don't know." They lament over the fact that they don't know anybody important. They feel it is a requirement for getting a job. They don't realize that they have skills beyond what they learned in the classroom. I tell them they should write down all the things they are able to do. Take stock of who they know and what they are able to do. Hopefully along the way, they'll get an epiphany. Eureka!

The ting behind two is definitely more than three.

What you perceive may be the covering of the real thing. As one peels away the layers of the story, what one finds most often are feelings of fear, anxiety and helplessness. These emotions block you from seeing the threes, the fours or the fives behind the twos of life.

Our emotions envelope us into a freeze. We cannot move beyond the known. It is difficult for a young man in Foya to perceive that he will ascend to the highest office in the land. It is hard for a young lady, who has no money to pay fees at the government school, to perceive that she will attend the most prestigious and expensive university; but these things happen all the time to others.

Chapter Seven

LIBERIANISM

"You See Baboon Teeth You Think He Laughing, Not Knowing He Crying"

Every time you see someone who appears to be happy, does not mean they are. We are good at hiding our real selves or putting on masks to cover up.

It has to do with "putting on your big girl panties" or "manning up".

No matter what's going on with you, don't let others see it. This is true in many circumstances, when you're with strangers, when you don't feel safe with your disclosure, when you don't understand the event or circumstance yourself so it's hard to explain it to someone else. There are a few cases, though, where this may not be true.

****

We went to a church service recently and people were standing up to give thanks to God for "bringing them through". In the cases, they recounted things in their lives in the past year that they felt God had done for them.

One lady talked about having no money to put her children in school. As she spoke I could see the pain in her eyes. Her voice trembled as she recalled not having enough food or money to take care of her family. Obviously she is a single mom with a job that pays little; possibly a backyard garden like everyone else in her village.

However she found the courage to announce to the world (well, the congregation) that she had been going through hard times. She was joyful that she came through but the worry was not over, the stress continued. She was not asking for money or sympathy. She was just happy that she had managed.

This story has stayed with me for a long time. I was touched by what she said but I also felt ashamed that we did not know what she was going through. Even though I had sat next to her many Sundays and we were in a women's group together I didn't even know her name (don't blame me, blame the age).

I almost went up to her to apologize for not being my brother's keeper. The lesson I got out was that I've got to do better.

Being my brother's keeper doesn't mean that I know all of my brother (or sister's) secrets. I think it means being aware of others and looking beyond their outer masks. It means saying hello and smiling at people around you so that they're comfortable enough with you to broach these uncomfortable subjects.

My friend Gloria was a happy person. Gloria and I were neighbors for about four years. We spent a lot of time together in her house. I went over to her house more often than she came to mine but that was because I was comfortable sitting on her bed and chewing the fat.

Recently, Gloria died, less than six months after she retired and left the neighborhood. The reason she died was an illness that must have been with her for a while.

While I think of Gloria I have to admire that even though she may have been in pain during talks, she never showed it. We only now remember that in the last few months she complained of gas pain, nothing more. Gloria is another example of *baboon showing his teeth.*

We have to be sensitive to the circumstances of the people around us. Even though someone may not voice what is deep in their hearts, we must be ready that when they do, we have a comforting heart and willing ears.

Author's Note

I always had a dream to do something about the abundance of fruits in my native Liberia. Now that dream has finally come through as a Co-Owner of *Fruit Fusion by KATE Industries*, a fruit juice company in Liberia.

I am a great believer of books. As an awkward, shy (aren't we all!) preteen, I escaped to our living room (why was it called that when no one ever 'lived' there? It was the most formal room in the house) where there were these floor-to-ceiling bookshelves. My favorite books were the World of Knowledge series which held stories, fiction and non-fiction. I remember curling up in the soft couch and spending hours living in other worlds. Life was simpler.

My inspiration for writing comes from my mother who is also an author. In her professional life she wrote many reports and essays but I was vividly surprised when I read her fiction. She had imagination and that made me proud.

The most favorite moments of my life have been being a mother to Richard, Bobby and Vanessa.

However, because I'm an educator I have worked with teens and tweens for over 25 years and as a result, my extended family has grown abundantly.

THE END

About the Author

Lovette Azango Tucker wears many hats. Her most favorite is being mother to Richard, Bobby and Vanessa. She has worked with teens and tweens for over 25 years. She has been a teacher, mentor, career counselor and a helping hand to young people. She loves working with the youth.

Her passion for mentoring young people about their lives and their careers is evidenced by the question she frequently asks, "What are you going to do with the rest of your life?"

Lovette always had a dream to do something about the abundance of fruits in her native Liberia. Now that dream has finally come through. She is Co-Owner of *Fruit Fusion by KATE Industries*, a fruit juice company in Liberia.

Her first book, **Street Beat**, a young adult fiction, is a collection of short stories.